For Dawn J.O.

To Lindsey and Rabbit from the girls x L.G.

# OXFORD
### UNIVERSITY PRESS

Great Clarendon Street, Oxford OX2 6DP

Oxford University Press is a department of the University of Oxford.
It furthers the University's objective of excellence in research, scholarship,
and education by publishing worldwide in

Oxford   New York

Auckland   Cape Town   Dar es Salaam   Hong Kong   Karachi
Kuala Lumpur   Madrid   Melbourne   Mexico City   Nairobi
New Delhi   Shanghai   Taipei   Toronto

With offices in

Argentina   Austria   Brazil   Chile   Czech Republic   France   Greece
Guatemala   Hungary   Italy   Japan   Poland   Portugal   Singapore
South Korea   Switzerland   Thailand   Turkey   Ukraine   Vietnam

Oxford is a registered trade mark of Oxford University Press
in the UK and in certain other countries

Text © Jan Ormerod 2005
Illustrations © Lindsey Gardiner 2005

British Library Cataloguing in Publication Data

Data available

ISBN-13: 978-0-19-279140-5 (paperback)
ISBN-10: 0-19-279140-0 (paperback)
ISBN-13: 978-0-19-271988-1 (paperback with audio CD)
ISBN-10: 0-19-271988-2 (paperback with audio CD)

5  7  9  10  8  6  4

Printed in China

# Doing the Animal BOP

Jan Ormerod and Lindsey Gardiner

IF you like to **dance**
and you sometimes **sing,**

why don't
you do the
animal thing?

Put your heels together,

and waddle along.

Go Craak Craak Craak – it's the **penguin** song!

High stepping knees and feathers that bounce-

flim-flam flutter to the **ostrich** flounce.

Jump and wiggle to the monkey bop.

Then go hee-haw hee-haw, too!

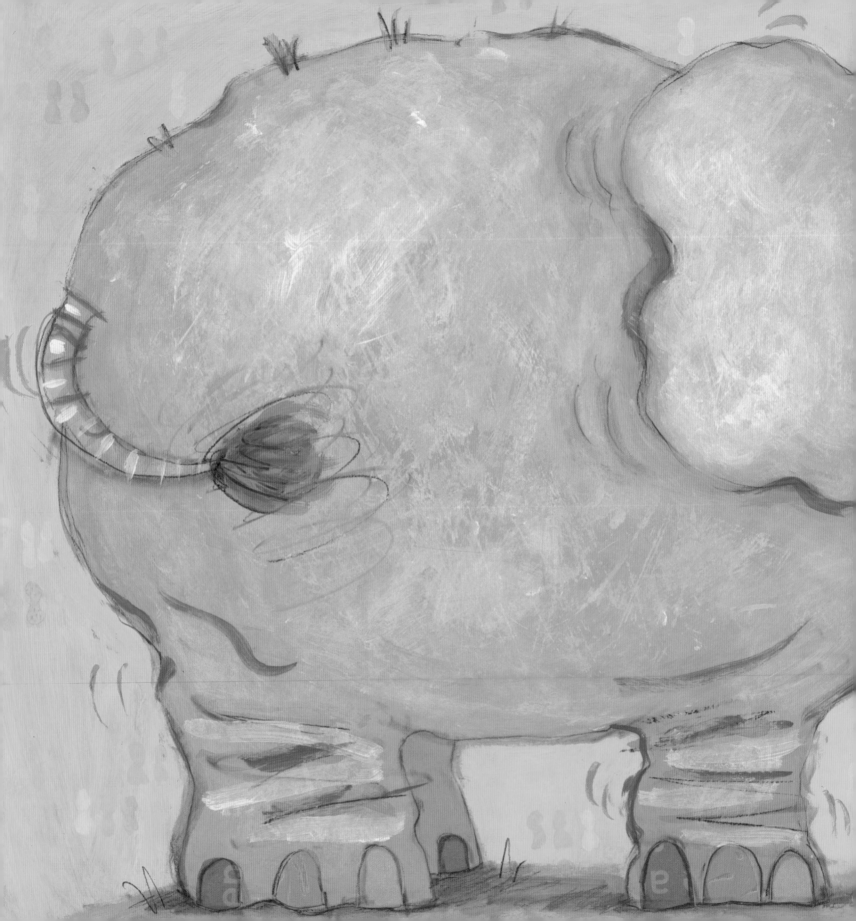

Wave one ARM.

STOMP your feet.

Trudge along to the elephant beat.

Move **one** leg.

A chicken can **peck** . . .

... and a chicken can **CLUCK**.

But I think it's more fun
being a **duck** ...

The duck does a **waddle**

on his **FLIP-FLAP** feet,

so **swing** your bottom

to the

**quack-quack** beat.

Roar and rage,

it's a rhino romp!

All the **COW** can do is chew.

So let's end up with a great big

mmmooooooooooOOO

mooooooooo